STAR WARS®

INFINITIES
A NEW HOPE

VOLUME THREE

Script **CHRIS WARNER**	Pencils and Inks **AL RIO**
Co-Inks **NEIL NELSON**	Colors **DAVE McCAIG**
Lettering **STEVE DUTRO**	Cover Art **TONY HARRIS** with **CHRIS BLYTHE**

Luke Skywalker's proton torpedo failed to destroy the Death Star, and the Rebellion was defeated at the Battle of Yavin.

Luke received instructions from the ghost of Obi-Wan Kenobi, and he, Han Solo, and Chewbacca made their way to the planet Dagobah. There they met the Jedi Master Yoda, who began training Luke for the trials that lay ahead.

But Luke was not the only one being trained. Princess Leia, captured by Darth Vader, was introduced to the power of the Force, and Vader began to groom her to become his apprentice. That was five years ago . . .

THE *STAR WARS INFINITIES* SERIES ASKS THE QUESTION: WHAT IF ONE THING HAPPENED DIFFERENTLY FROM WHAT WE SAW IN THE CLASSIC FILMS?

DARK HORSE COMICS

Visit us at www.abdopublishing.com

Reinforced library bound edition published in 2011 by Spotlight, a division of the ABDO Group, 8000 West 78th Street, Edina, Minnesota 55439. Spotlight produces high-quality reinforced library bound editions for schools and libraries. Published by agreement with Dark Horse Comics, Inc., and Lucasfilm Ltd.

Printed in the United States of America, North Mankato, Minnesota.
102010
012011
♻ This book contains at least 10% recycled materials.

Library of Congress Cataloging-in-Publication Data

Warner, Chris.
  A new hope / script, Chris Warner ; art, Drew Johnson. -- Reinforced library bound ed.
      v. cm. -- (Star Wars. Infinities)
  ISBN 978-1-59961-845-6 (vol. 1) -- ISBN 978-1-59961-846-3 (vol. 2) -- ISBN 978-1-59961-847-0 (vol. 3) -- ISBN 978-1-59961-848-7 (vol. 4)
  1. Graphic novels. [1. Graphic novels. 2. Science fiction.] I. Johnson, Drew, ill. II. Title.
  PZ7.7.W37New 2011
  741.5'973--dc22

                          2010020246

All Spotlight books have reinforced library bindings and are manufactured in the United States of America.

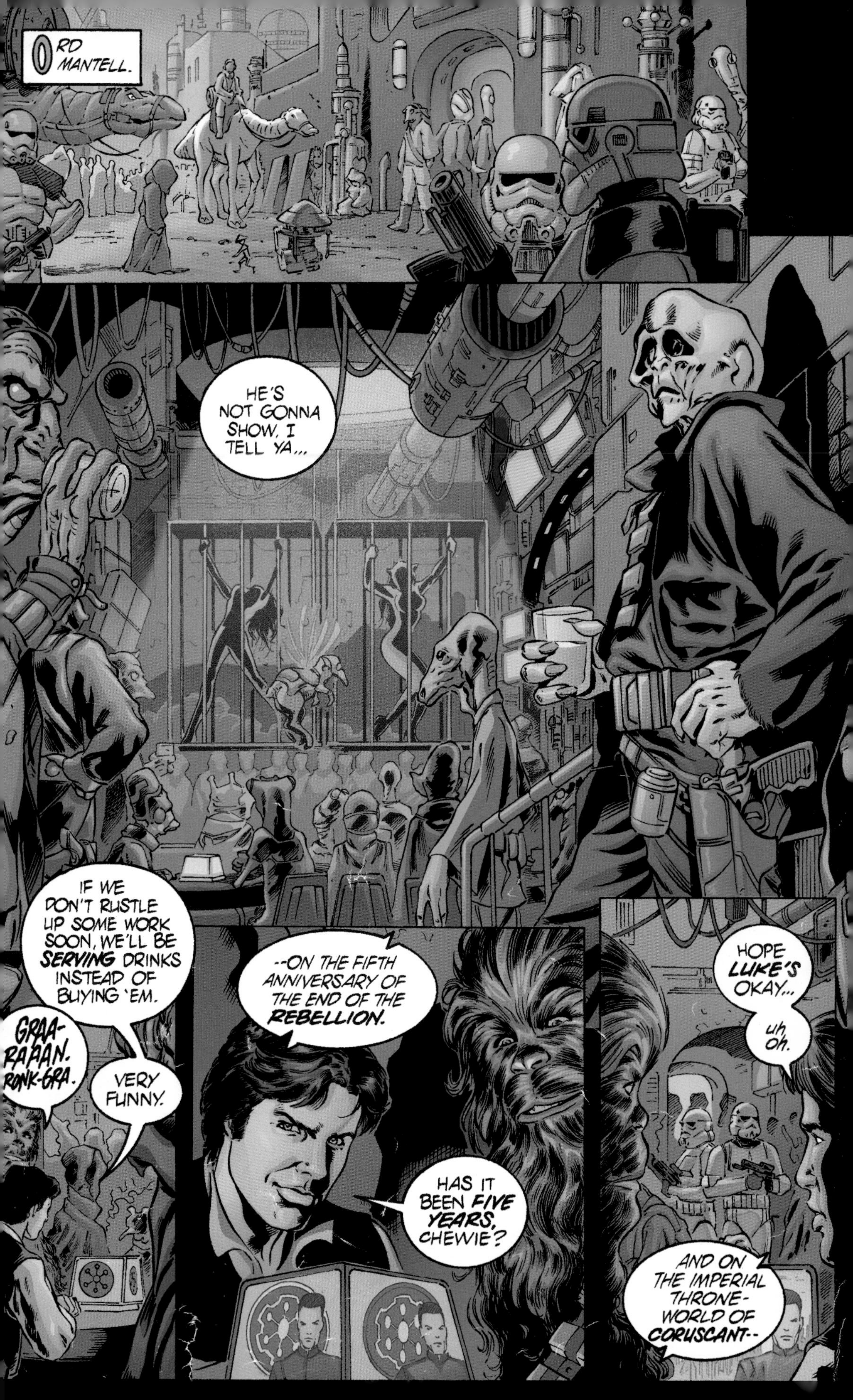
ORD MANTELL.
HE'S NOT GONNA SHOW, I TELL YA...
IF WE DON'T RUSTLE UP SOME WORK SOON, WE'LL BE SERVING DRINKS INSTEAD OF BUYING 'EM.
GRAA-RAAAN. RONK-GRA.
VERY FUNNY.
--ON THE FIFTH ANNIVERSARY OF THE END OF THE REBELLION.
HAS IT BEEN FIVE YEARS, CHEWIE?
HOPE LUKE'S OKAY...
uh oh.
AND ON THE IMPERIAL THRONE-WORLD OF CORUSCANT--

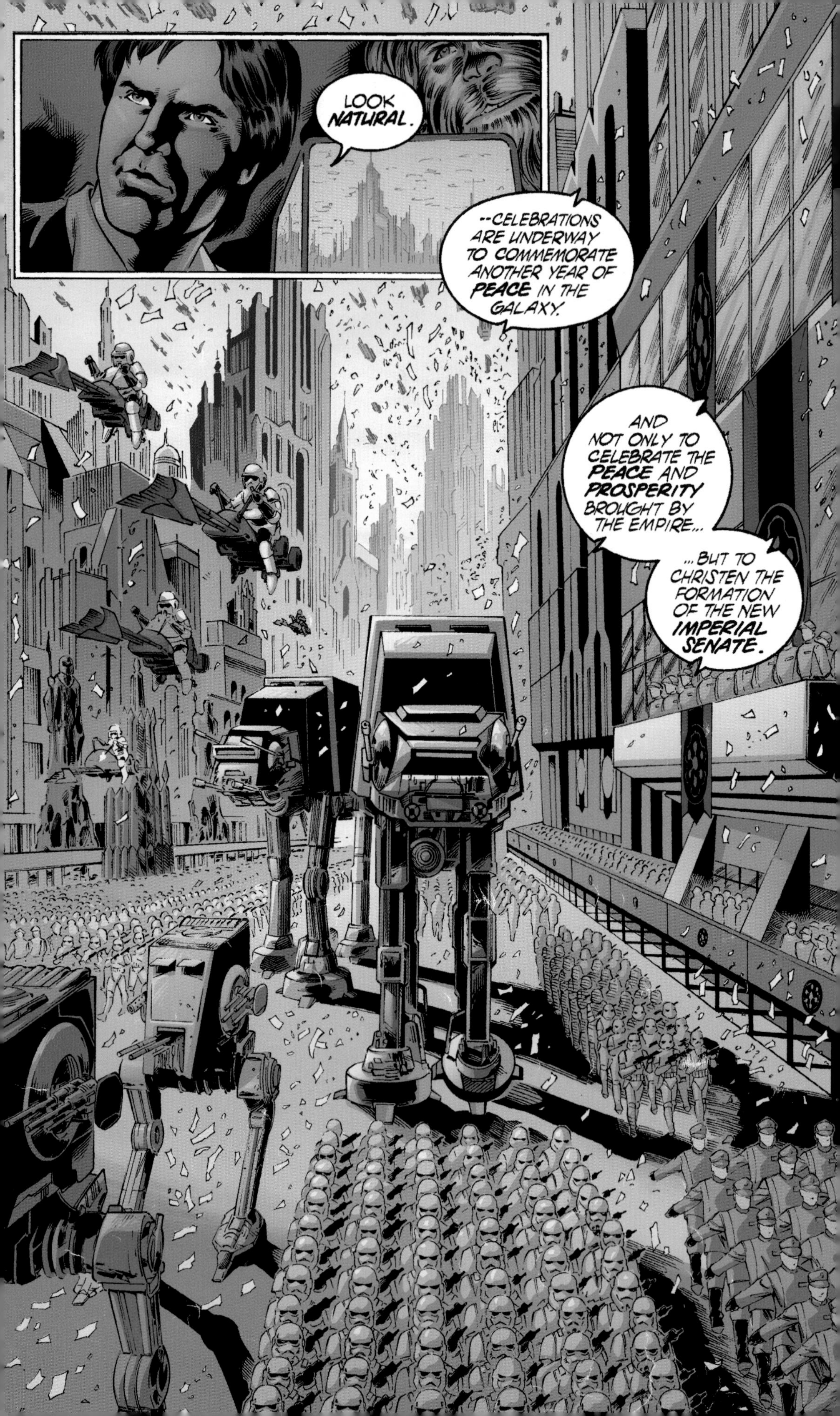
LOOK NATURAL.
--CELEBRATIONS ARE UNDERWAY TO COMMEMORATE ANOTHER YEAR OF PEACE IN THE GALAXY.
AND NOT ONLY TO CELEBRATE THE PEACE AND PROSPERITY BROUGHT BY THE EMPIRE...
...BUT TO CHRISTEN THE FORMATION OF THE NEW IMPERIAL SENATE.

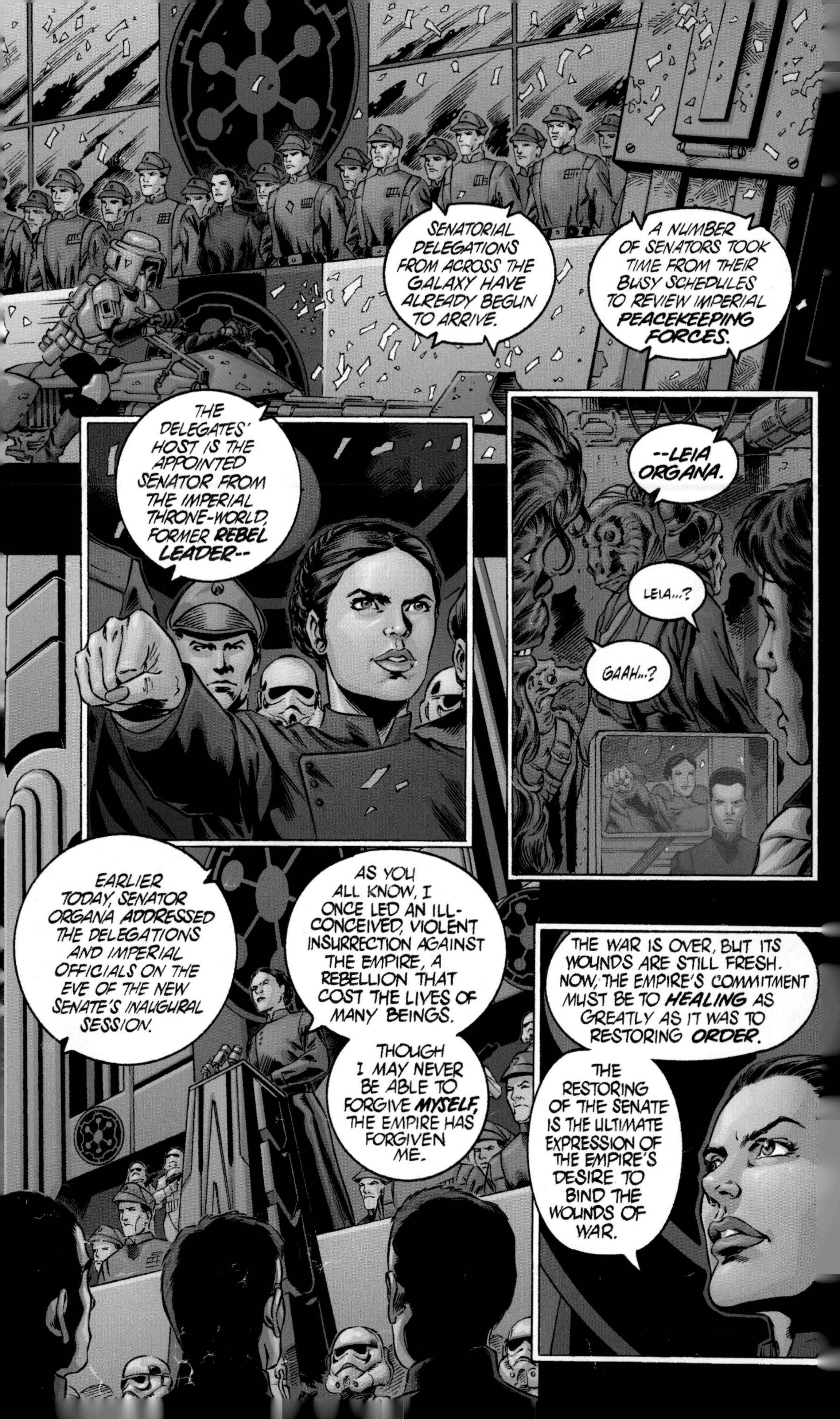

SENATORIAL DELEGATIONS FROM ACROSS THE GALAXY HAVE ALREADY BEGUN TO ARRIVE.
A NUMBER OF SENATORS TOOK TIME FROM THEIR BUSY SCHEDULES TO REVIEW IMPERIAL PEACEKEEPING FORCES.
THE DELEGATES' HOST IS THE APPOINTED SENATOR FROM THE IMPERIAL THRONE-WORLD, FORMER REBEL LEADER--
--LEIA ORGANA.
LEIA...?
GAAH...?
EARLIER TODAY, SENATOR ORGANA ADDRESSED THE DELEGATIONS AND IMPERIAL OFFICIALS ON THE EVE OF THE NEW SENATE'S INAUGURAL SESSION.
AS YOU ALL KNOW, I ONCE LED AN ILL-CONCEIVED, VIOLENT INSURRECTION AGAINST THE EMPIRE, A REBELLION THAT COST THE LIVES OF MANY BEINGS.
THOUGH I MAY NEVER BE ABLE TO FORGIVE MYSELF, THE EMPIRE HAS FORGIVEN ME.
THE WAR IS OVER, BUT ITS WOUNDS ARE STILL FRESH. NOW, THE EMPIRE'S COMMITMENT MUST BE TO HEALING AS GREATLY AS IT WAS TO RESTORING ORDER.
THE RESTORING OF THE SENATE IS THE ULTIMATE EXPRESSION OF THE EMPIRE'S DESIRE TO BIND THE WOUNDS OF WAR.

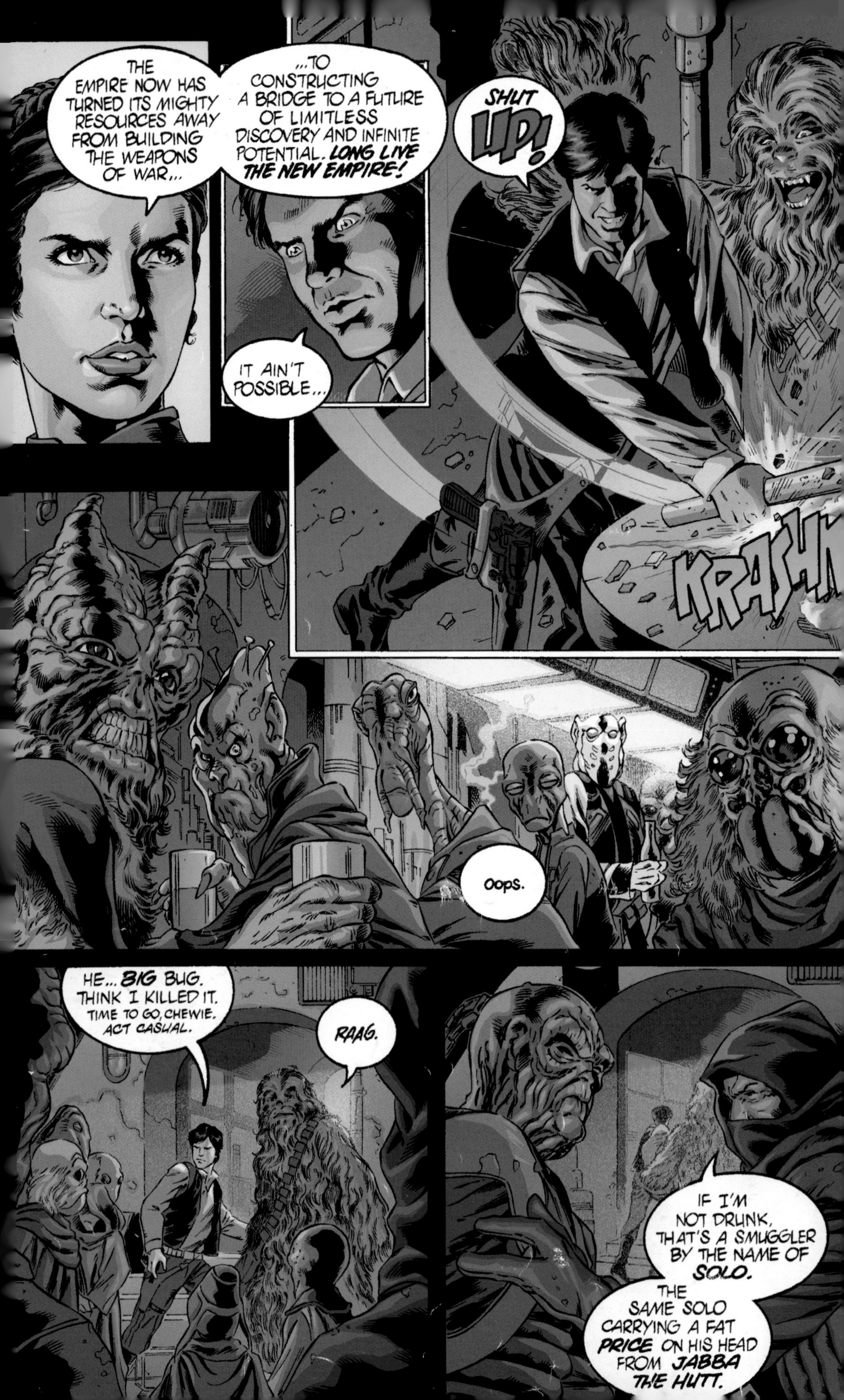
THE EMPIRE NOW HAS TURNED ITS MIGHTY RESOURCES AWAY FROM BUILDING THE WEAPONS OF WAR...
...TO CONSTRUCTING A BRIDGE TO A FUTURE OF LIMITLESS DISCOVERY AND INFINITE POTENTIAL. LONG LIVE THE NEW EMPIRE!
IT AIN'T POSSIBLE...
SHUT UP!
KRASH
Oops.
HE... BIG BUG. THINK I KILLED IT. TIME TO GO, CHEWIE. ACT CASUAL.
RAAG.
IF I'M NOT DRUNK, THAT'S A SMUGGLER BY THE NAME OF SOLO.
THE SAME SOLO CARRYING A FAT PRICE ON HIS HEAD FROM JABBA THE HUTT.

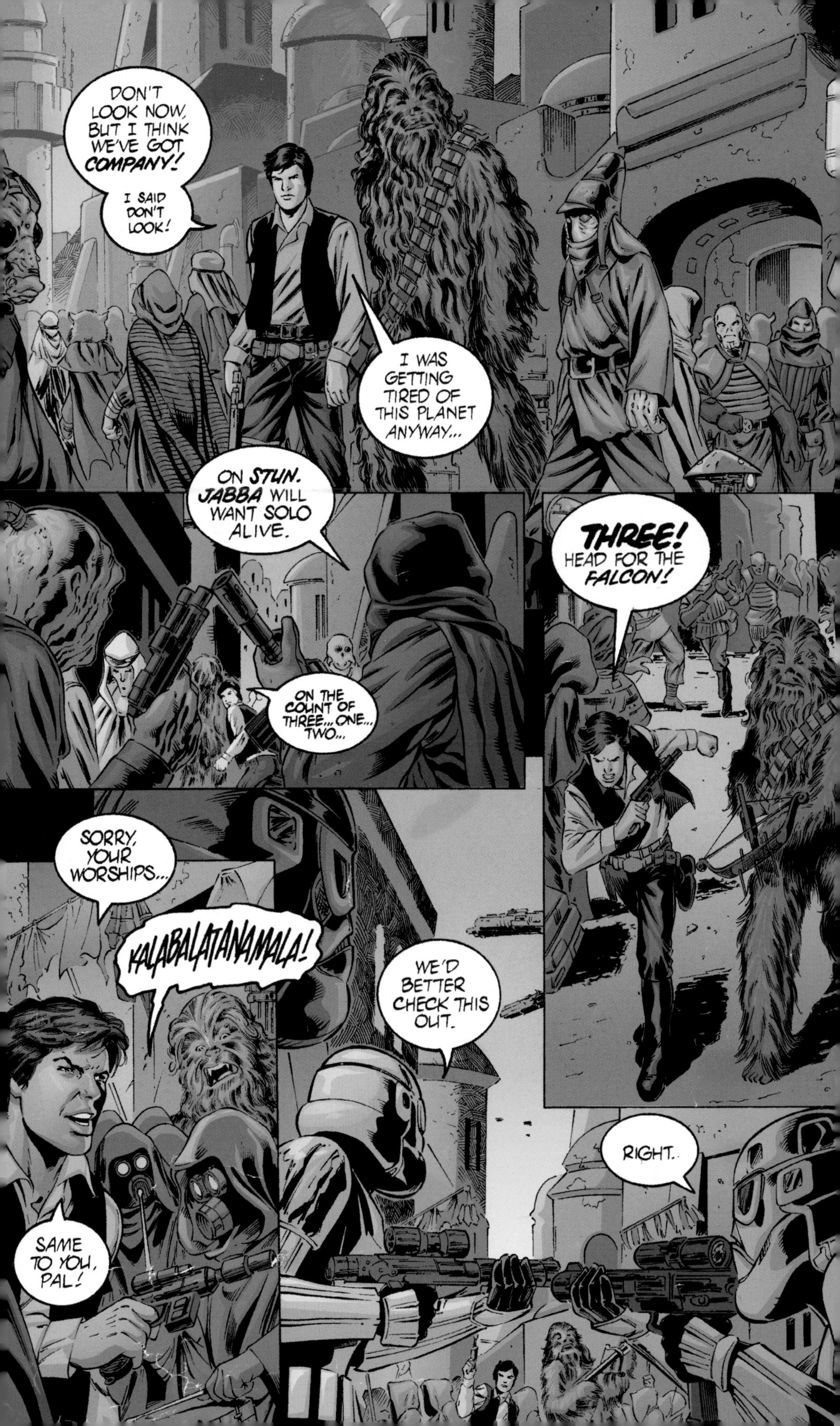
DON'T LOOK NOW, BUT I THINK WE'VE GOT COMPANY!
I SAID DON'T LOOK!
I WAS GETTING TIRED OF THIS PLANET ANYWAY...
ON STUN. JABBA WILL WANT SOLO ALIVE.
ON THE COUNT OF THREE... ONE... TWO...
THREE! HEAD FOR THE FALCON!
SORRY, YOUR WORSHIPS...
KALABALATANAMALA!
SAME TO YOU, PAL!
WE'D BETTER CHECK THIS OUT.
RIGHT.

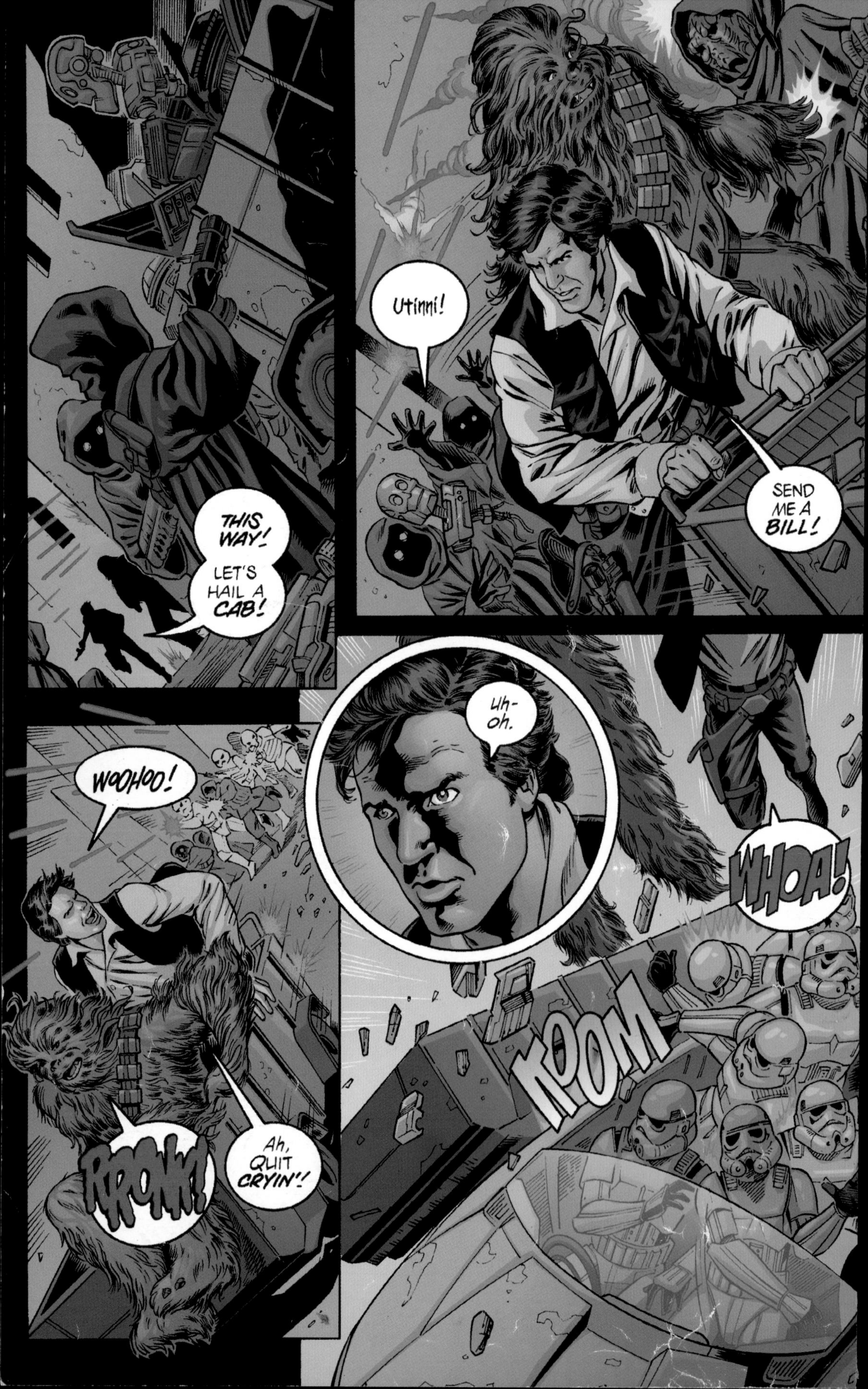
THIS WAY!
LET'S HAIL A CAB!
Utinni!
SEND ME A BILL!
WOOHOO!
RRONK!
Ah, QUIT CRYIN'!
Uh-oh.
WHOA!
KOOM

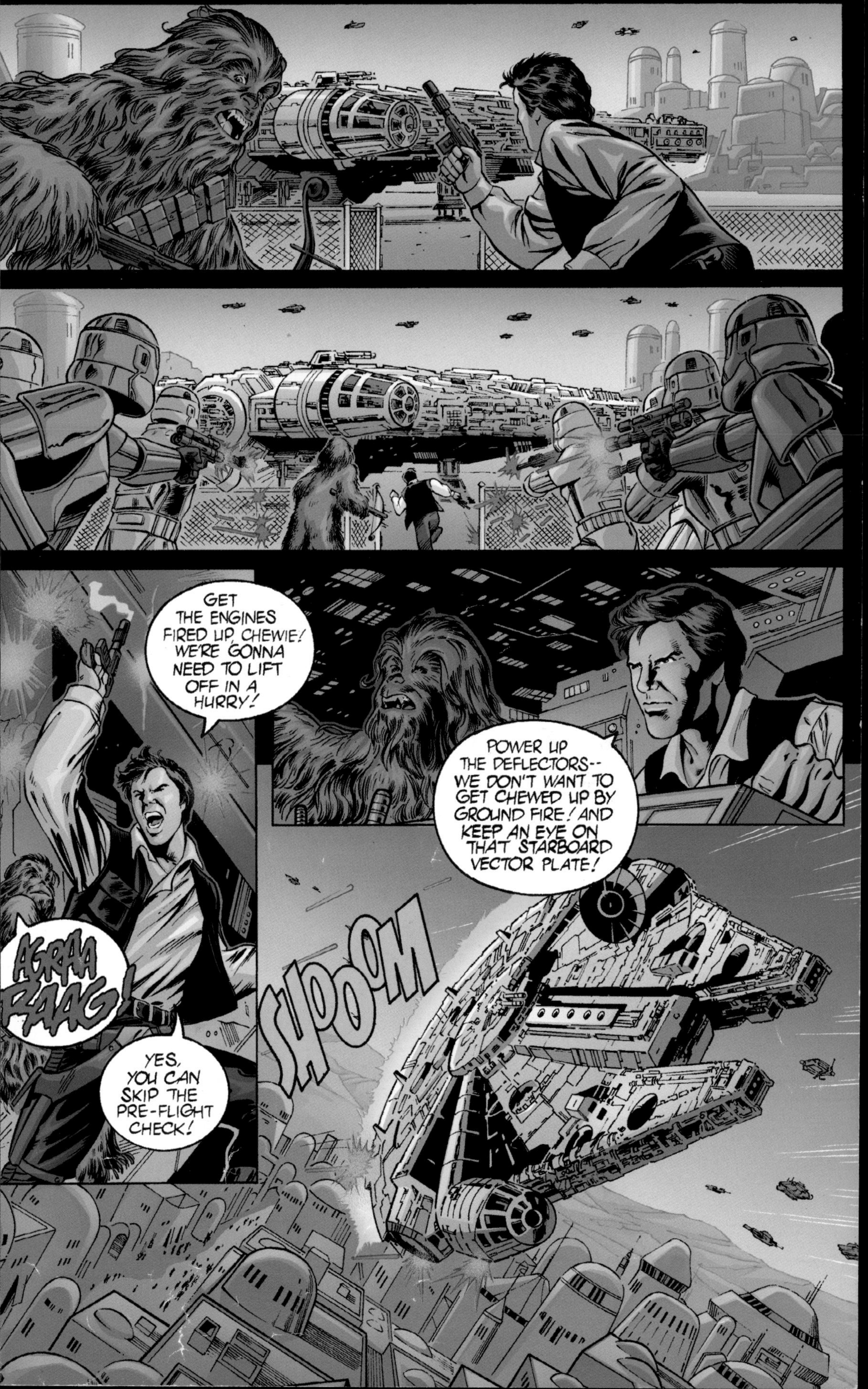
GET THE ENGINES FIRED UP, CHEWIE! WE'RE GONNA NEED TO LIFT OFF IN A HURRY!
AGRAAA RAAAG!
YES, YOU CAN SKIP THE PRE-FLIGHT CHECK!
POWER UP THE DEFLECTORS-- WE DON'T WANT TO GET CHEWED UP BY GROUND FIRE! AND KEEP AN EYE ON THAT STARBOARD VECTOR PLATE!
SHOOOM

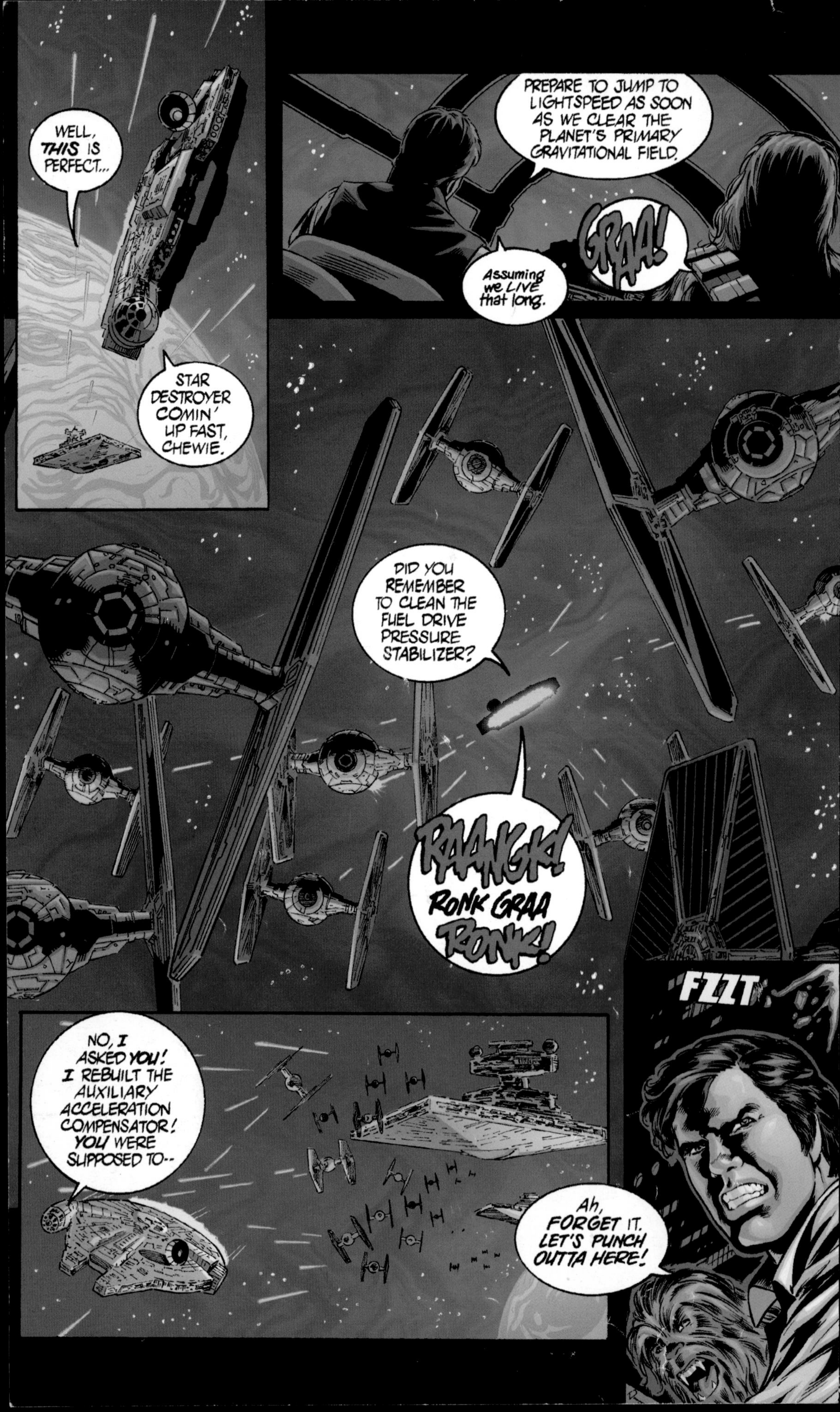
WELL, THIS IS PERFECT...
STAR DESTROYER COMIN' UP FAST, CHEWIE.
PREPARE TO JUMP TO LIGHTSPEED AS SOON AS WE CLEAR THE PLANET'S PRIMARY GRAVITATIONAL FIELD.
GRAA!
Assuming we LIVE that long.
DID YOU REMEMBER TO CLEAN THE FUEL DRIVE PRESSURE STABILIZER?
RAANGK! RONK GRAA RONK!
FZZT
NO, I ASKED YOU! I REBUILT THE AUXILIARY ACCELERATION COMPENSATOR! YOU WERE SUPPOSED TO--
Ah, FORGET IT. LET'S PUNCH OUTTA HERE!

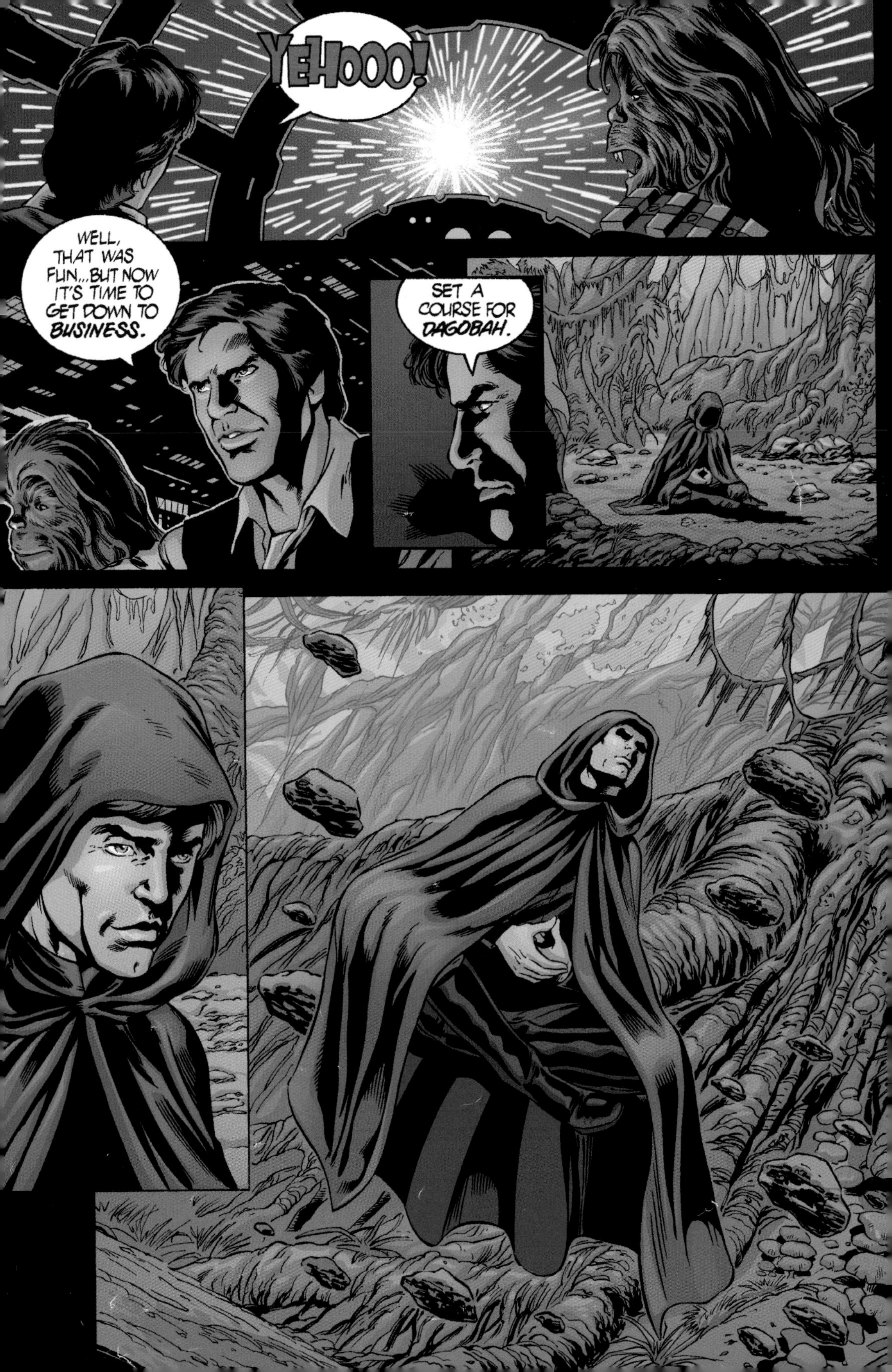
YEHOOO!
WELL, THAT WAS FUN,...BUT NOW IT'S TIME TO GET DOWN TO **BUSINESS**.
SET A COURSE FOR **DAGOBAH**.

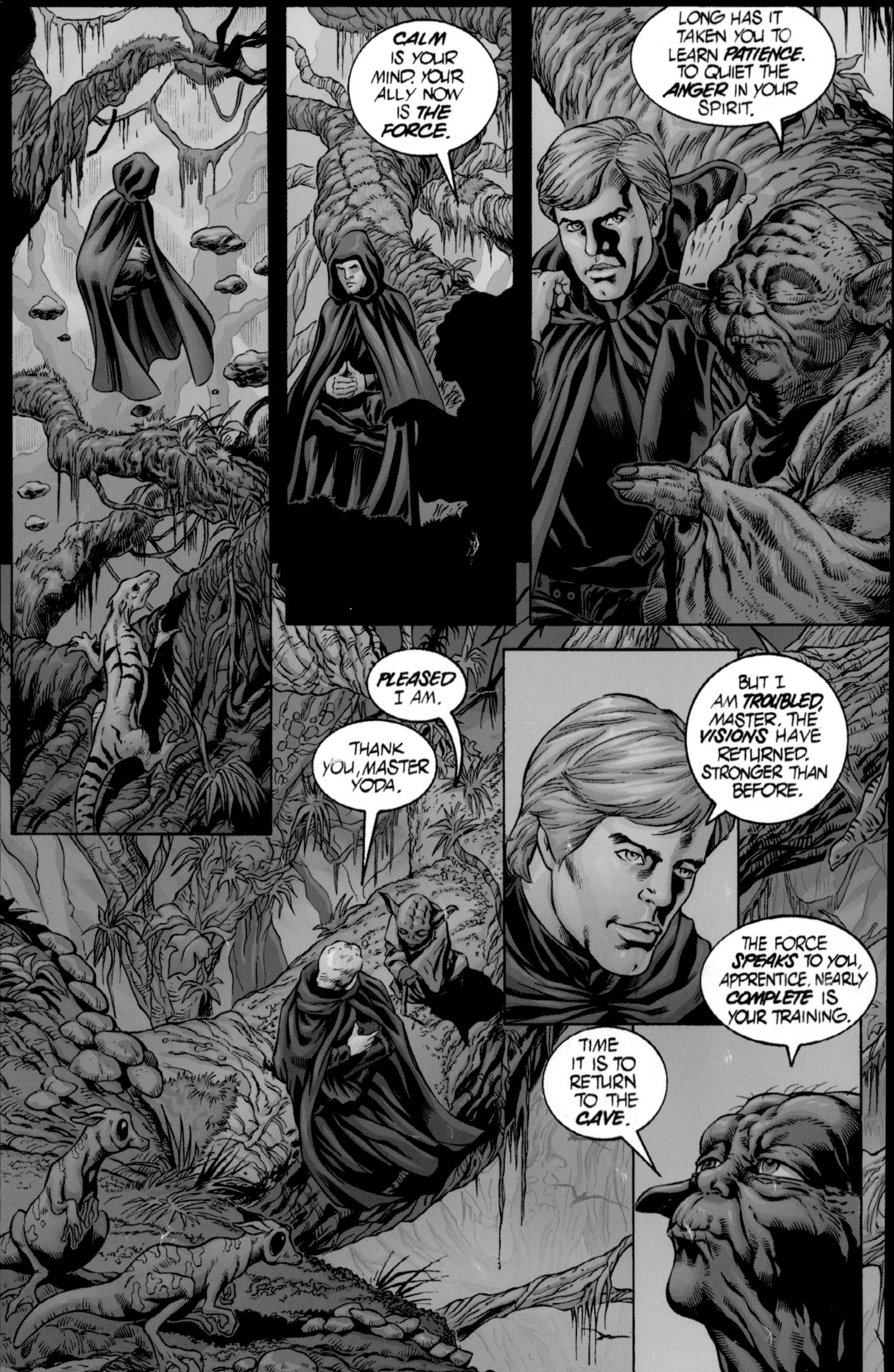
CALM IS YOUR MIND. YOUR ALLY NOW IS THE FORCE.
LONG HAS IT TAKEN YOU TO LEARN PATIENCE. TO QUIET THE ANGER IN YOUR SPIRIT.
PLEASED I AM.
THANK YOU, MASTER YODA.
BUT I AM TROUBLED, MASTER. THE VISIONS HAVE RETURNED. STRONGER THAN BEFORE.
THE FORCE SPEAKS TO YOU, APPRENTICE. NEARLY COMPLETE IS YOUR TRAINING.
TIME IT IS TO RETURN TO THE CAVE.

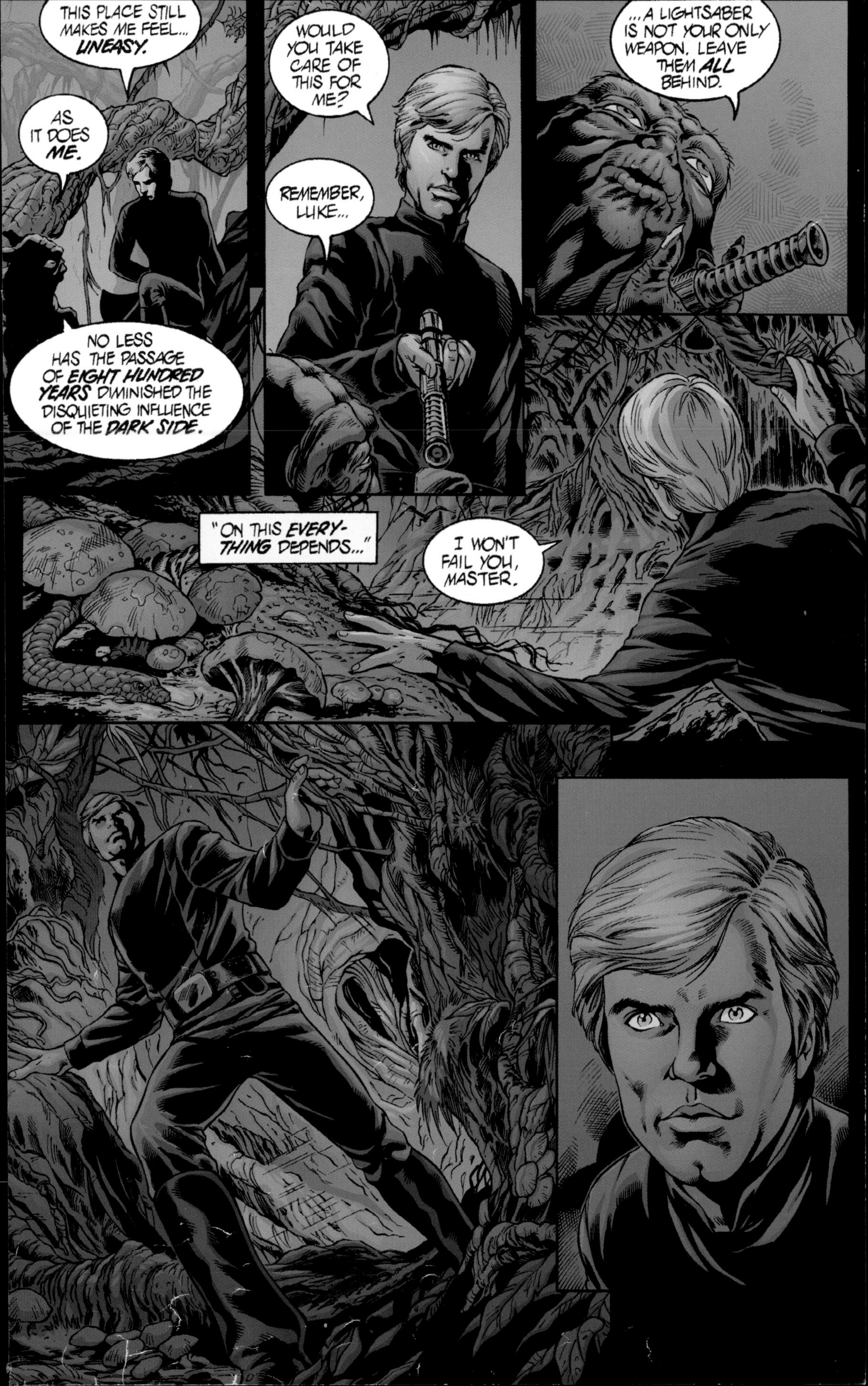
THIS PLACE STILL MAKES ME FEEL... UNEASY.
AS IT DOES ME.
NO LESS HAS THE PASSAGE OF EIGHT HUNDRED YEARS DIMINISHED THE DISQUIETING INFLUENCE OF THE DARK SIDE.
WOULD YOU TAKE CARE OF THIS FOR ME?
REMEMBER, LUKE...
...A LIGHTSABER IS NOT YOUR ONLY WEAPON. LEAVE THEM ALL BEHIND.
"ON THIS EVERY-THING DEPENDS..."
I WON'T FAIL YOU, MASTER.

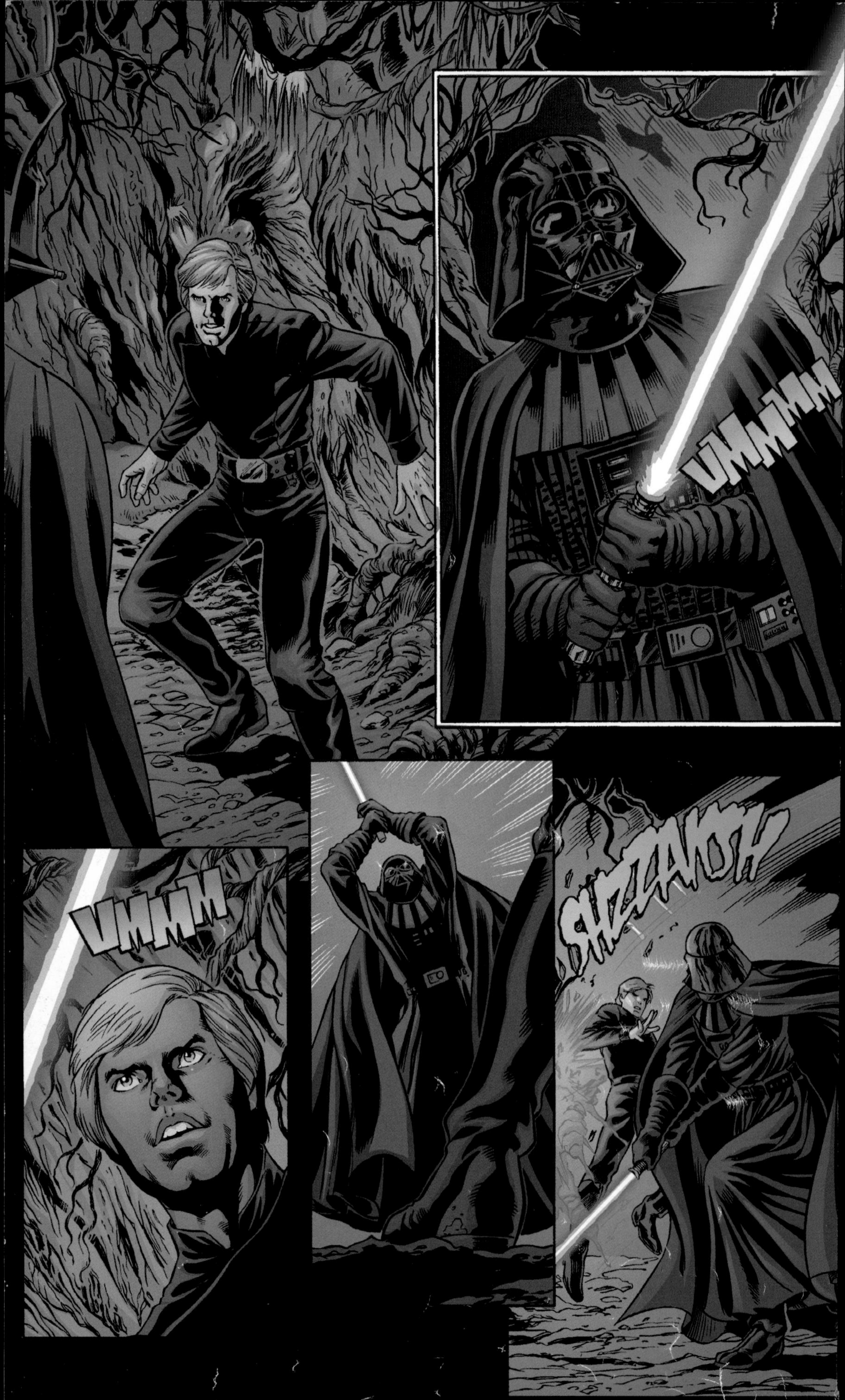

UMMMM
UMMM
SHZZAKOH

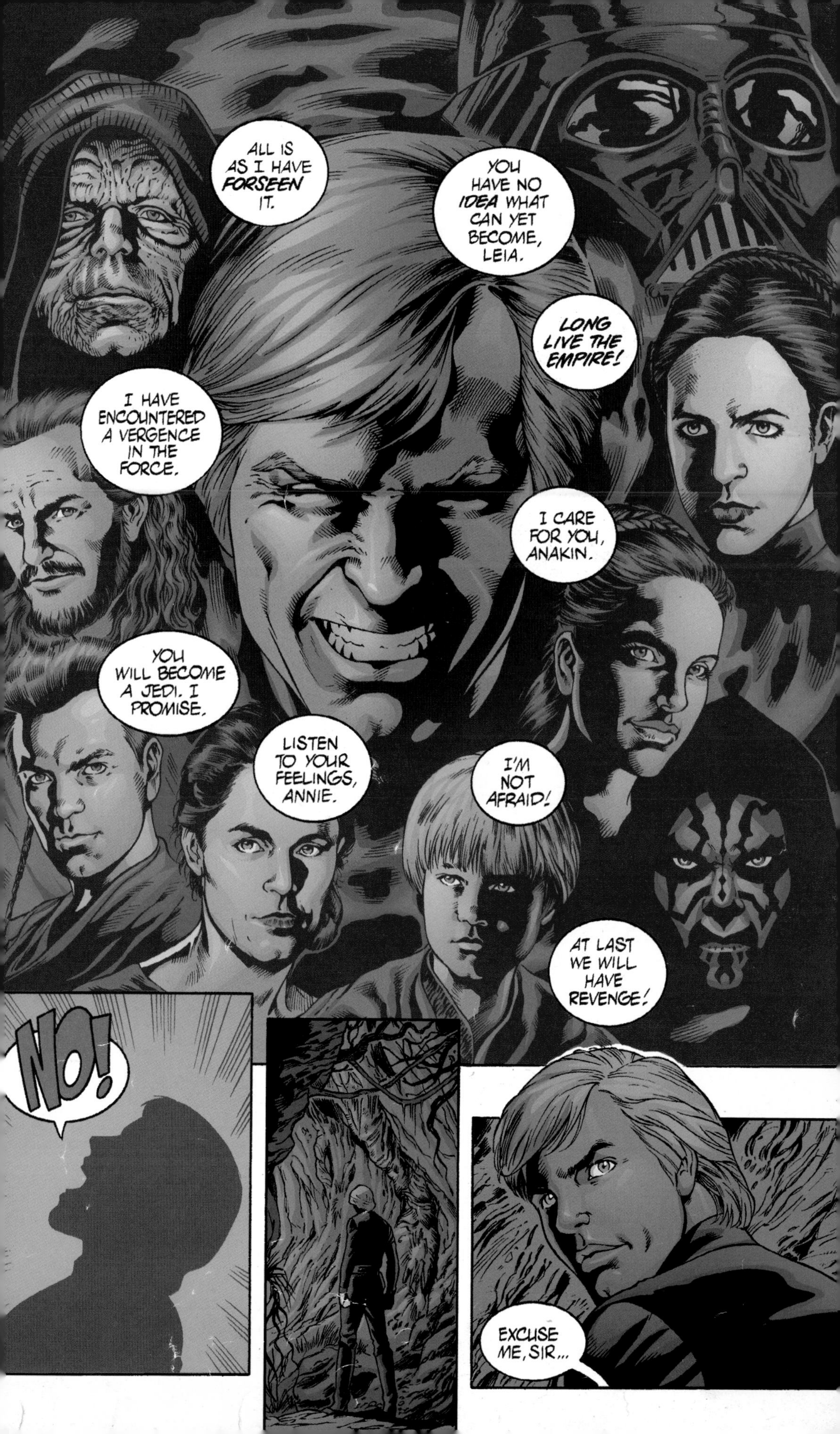

ALL IS AS I HAVE *FORSEEN* IT.
YOU HAVE NO *IDEA* WHAT CAN YET BECOME, LEIA.
LONG LIVE THE EMPIRE!
I HAVE ENCOUNTERED A VERGENCE IN THE FORCE.
I CARE FOR YOU, ANAKIN.
YOU WILL BECOME A JEDI. I PROMISE.
LISTEN TO YOUR FEELINGS, ANNIE.
I'M NOT AFRAID!
AT LAST WE WILL HAVE REVENGE!
NO!
EXCUSE ME, SIR...

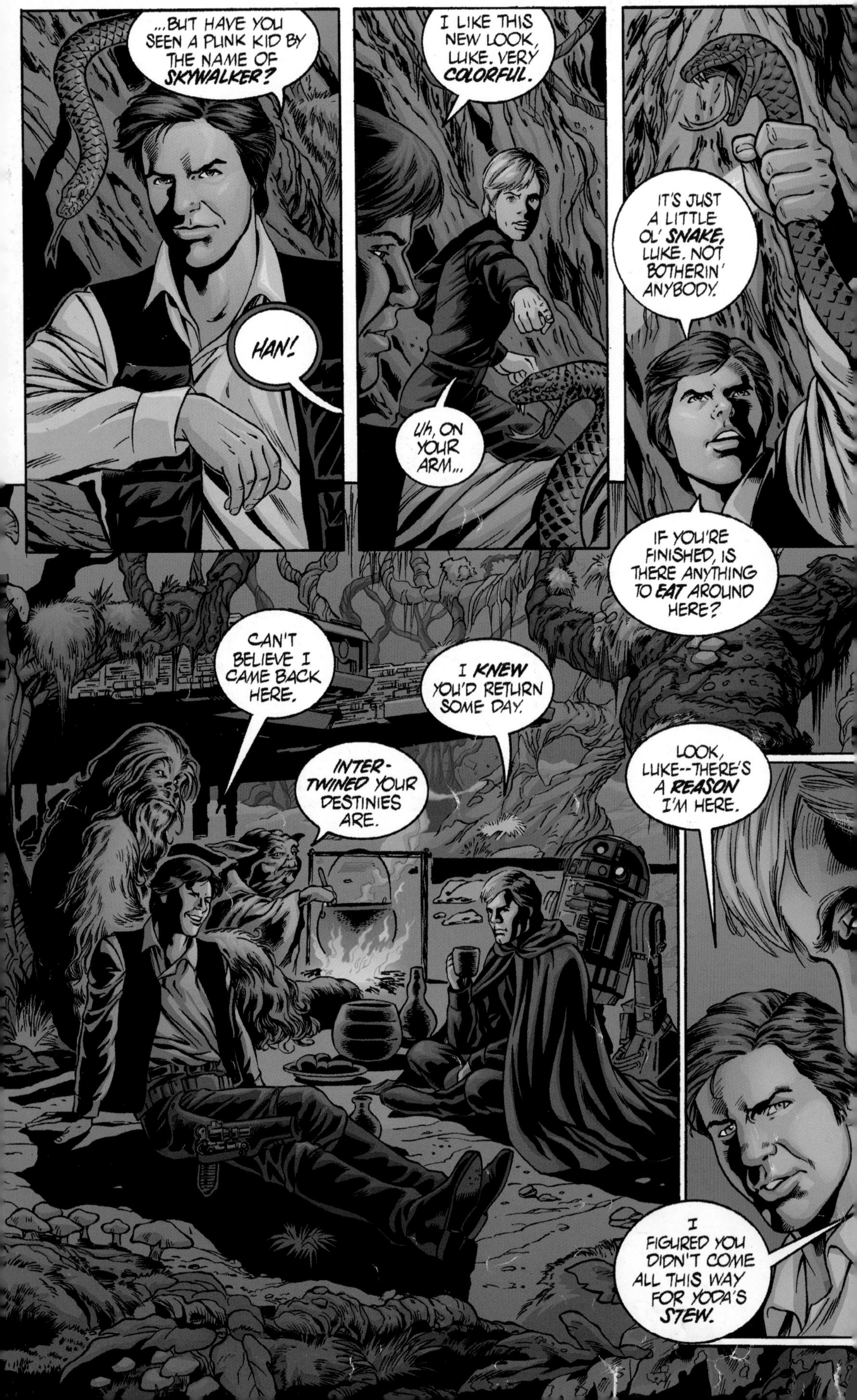
...BUT HAVE YOU SEEN A PUNK KID BY THE NAME OF SKYWALKER?
HAN!
I LIKE THIS NEW LOOK, LUKE. VERY COLORFUL.
Uh, ON YOUR ARM...
IT'S JUST A LITTLE OL' SNAKE, LUKE. NOT BOTHERIN' ANYBODY.
IF YOU'RE FINISHED, IS THERE ANYTHING TO EAT AROUND HERE?
CAN'T BELIEVE I CAME BACK HERE.
I KNEW YOU'D RETURN SOME DAY.
INTER-TWINED YOUR DESTINIES ARE.
LOOK, LUKE--THERE'S A REASON I'M HERE.
I FIGURED YOU DIDN'T COME ALL THIS WAY FOR YODA'S STEW.

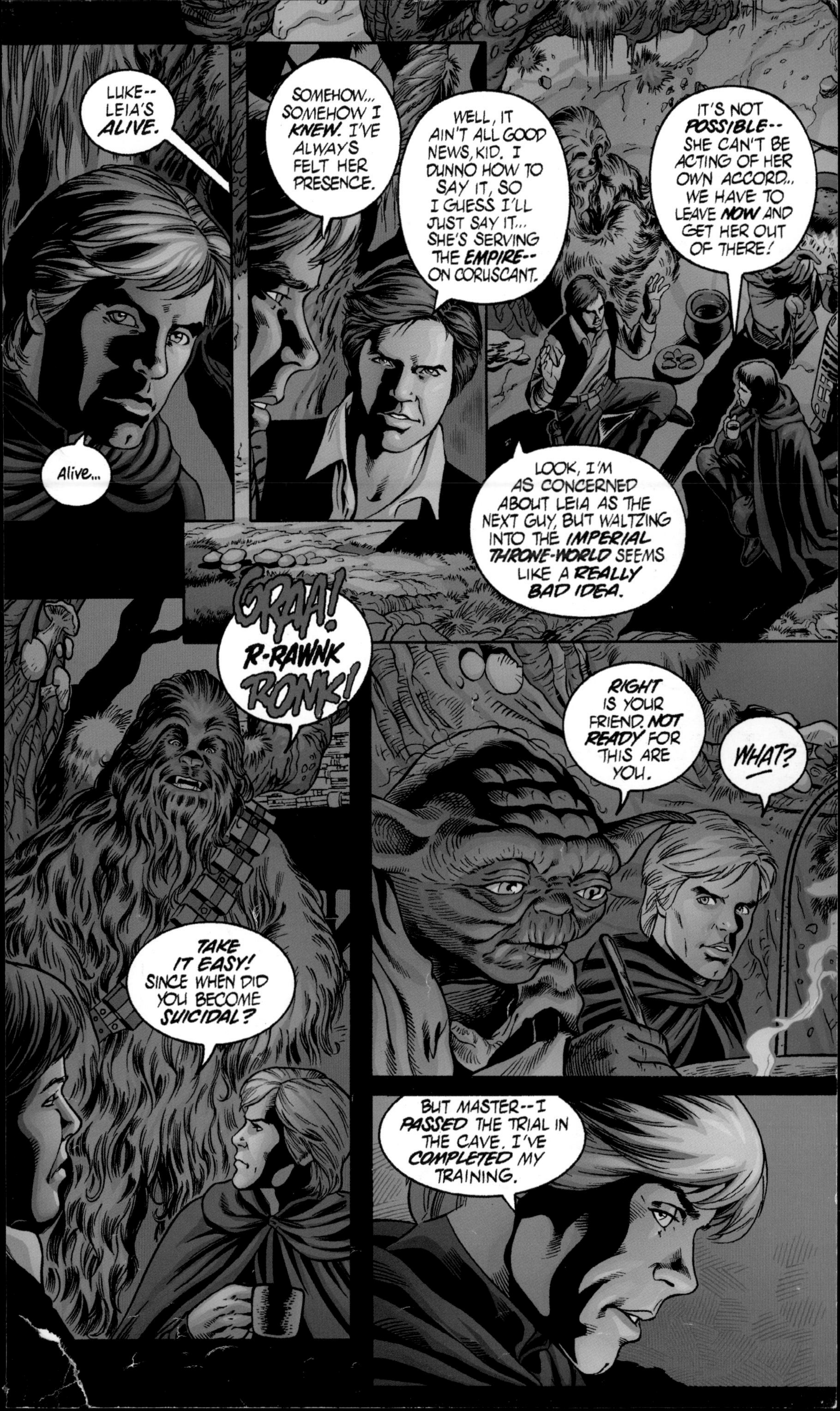

LUKE-- LEIA'S ALIVE.
Alive...
SOMEHOW... SOMEHOW I KNEW. I'VE ALWAYS FELT HER PRESENCE.
WELL, IT AIN'T ALL GOOD NEWS, KID. I DUNNO HOW TO SAY IT, SO I GUESS I'LL JUST SAY IT... SHE'S SERVING THE EMPIRE-- ON CORUSCANT.
IT'S NOT POSSIBLE-- SHE CAN'T BE ACTING OF HER OWN ACCORD... WE HAVE TO LEAVE NOW AND GET HER OUT OF THERE!
LOOK, I'M AS CONCERNED ABOUT LEIA AS THE NEXT GUY, BUT WALTZING INTO THE IMPERIAL THRONE-WORLD SEEMS LIKE A REALLY BAD IDEA.
GRAA! R-RAWNK RONK!
TAKE IT EASY! SINCE WHEN DID YOU BECOME SUICIDAL?
RIGHT IS YOUR FRIEND. NOT READY FOR THIS ARE YOU.
WHAT?
BUT MASTER--I PASSED THE TRIAL IN THE CAVE. I'VE COMPLETED MY TRAINING.

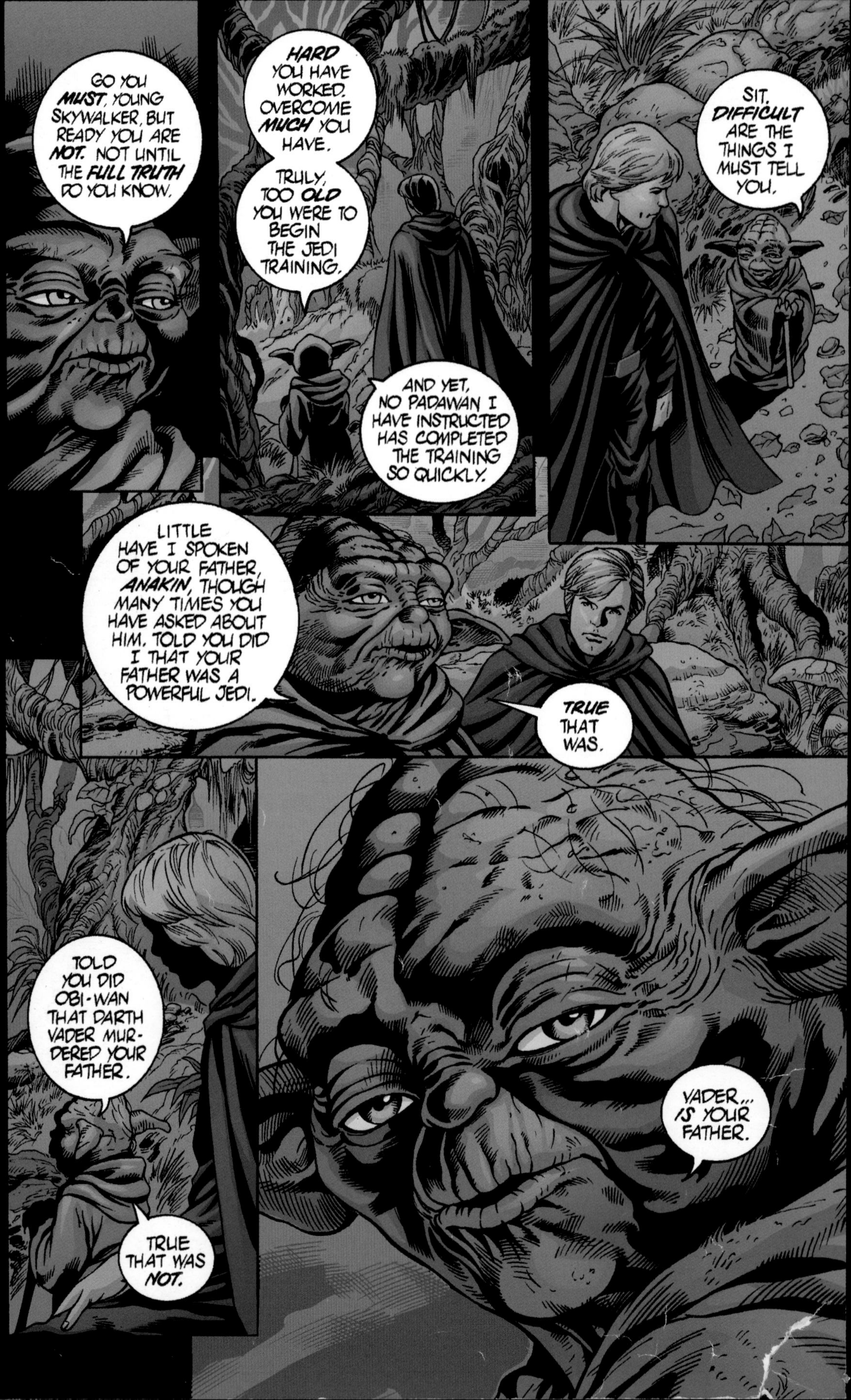
GO YOU MUST, YOUNG SKYWALKER, BUT READY YOU ARE NOT. NOT UNTIL THE FULL TRUTH DO YOU KNOW.
HARD YOU HAVE WORKED. OVERCOME MUCH YOU HAVE.
TRULY, TOO OLD YOU WERE TO BEGIN THE JEDI TRAINING.
AND YET, NO PADAWAN I HAVE INSTRUCTED HAS COMPLETED THE TRAINING SO QUICKLY.
SIT. DIFFICULT ARE THE THINGS I MUST TELL YOU.
LITTLE HAVE I SPOKEN OF YOUR FATHER, ANAKIN, THOUGH MANY TIMES YOU HAVE ASKED ABOUT HIM. TOLD YOU DID I THAT YOUR FATHER WAS A POWERFUL JEDI.
TRUE THAT WAS.
TOLD YOU DID OBI-WAN THAT DARTH VADER MURDERED YOUR FATHER.
TRUE THAT WAS NOT.
VADER... IS YOUR FATHER.

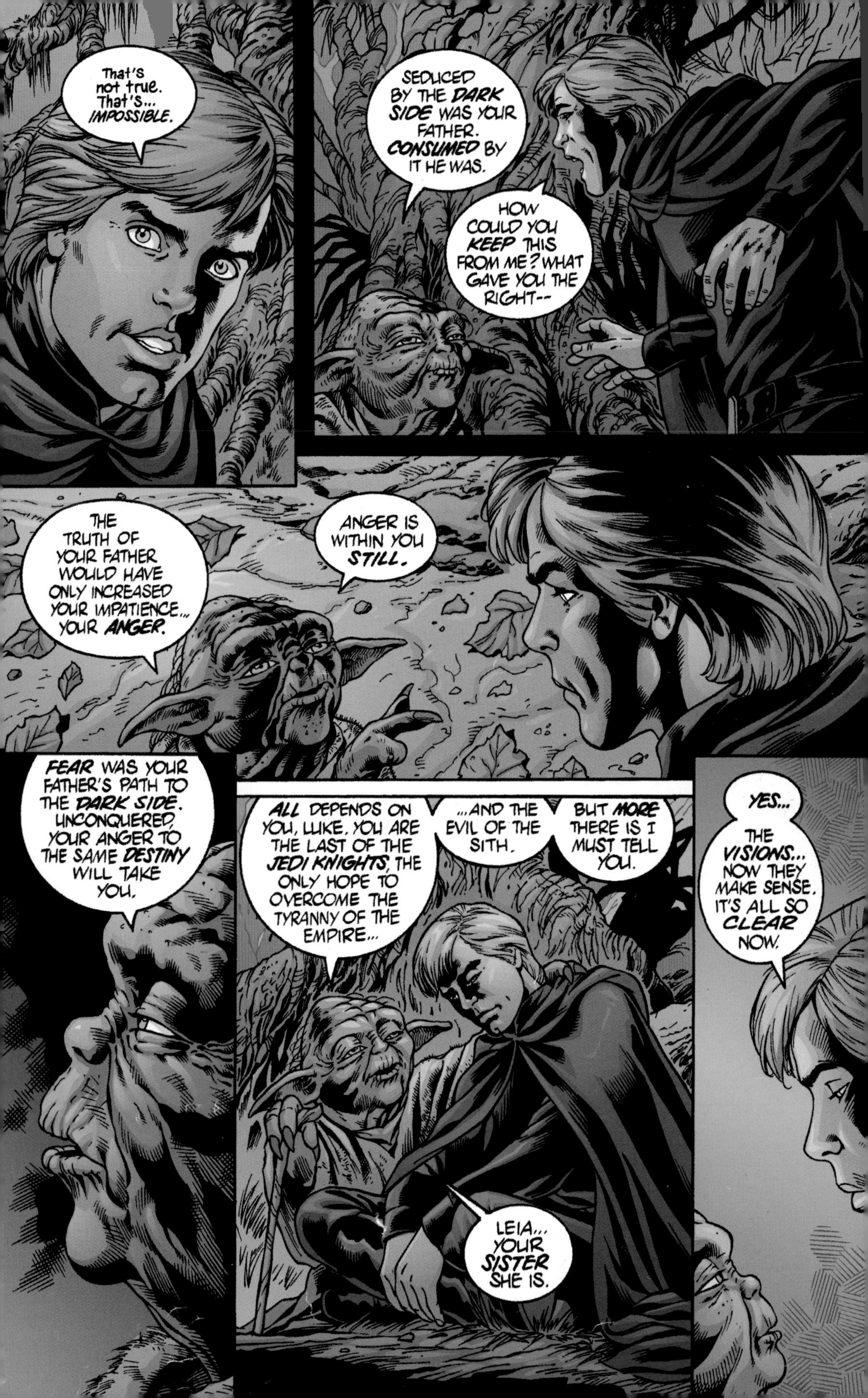
That's not true. That's... IMPOSSIBLE.
SEDUCED BY THE DARK SIDE WAS YOUR FATHER. CONSUMED BY IT HE WAS.
HOW COULD YOU KEEP THIS FROM ME? WHAT GAVE YOU THE RIGHT--
THE TRUTH OF YOUR FATHER WOULD HAVE ONLY INCREASED YOUR IMPATIENCE... YOUR ANGER.
ANGER IS WITHIN YOU STILL.
FEAR WAS YOUR FATHER'S PATH TO THE DARK SIDE. UNCONQUERED, YOUR ANGER TO THE SAME DESTINY WILL TAKE YOU.
ALL DEPENDS ON YOU, LUKE. YOU ARE THE LAST OF THE JEDI KNIGHTS, THE ONLY HOPE TO OVERCOME THE TYRANNY OF THE EMPIRE...
...AND THE EVIL OF THE SITH.
BUT MORE THERE IS I MUST TELL YOU.
LEIA... YOUR SISTER SHE IS.
YES...
THE VISIONS... NOW THEY MAKE SENSE. IT'S ALL SO CLEAR NOW.

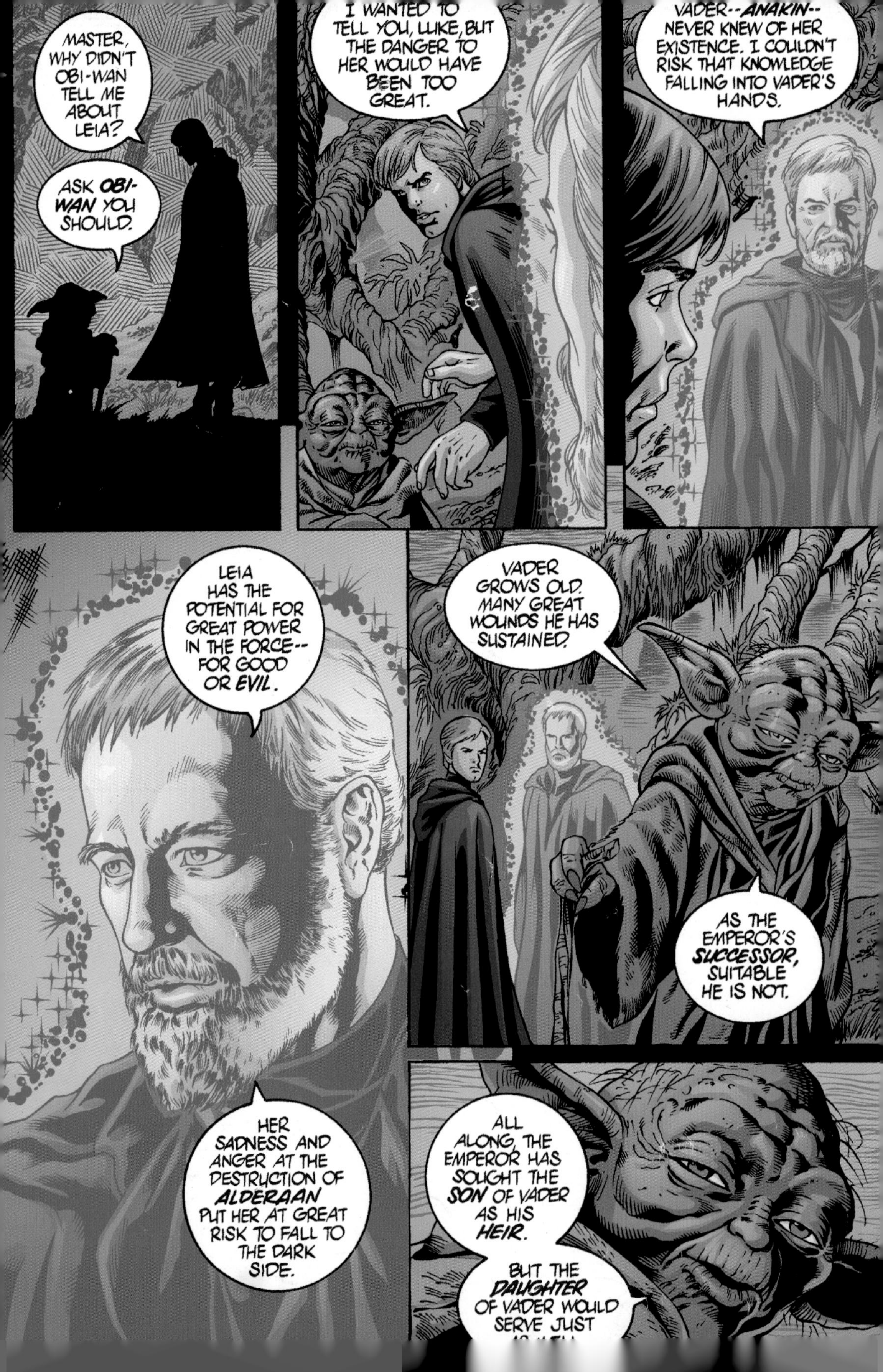
MASTER, WHY DIDN'T OBI-WAN TELL ME ABOUT LEIA?
ASK OBI-WAN YOU SHOULD.
I WANTED TO TELL YOU, LUKE, BUT THE DANGER TO HER WOULD HAVE BEEN TOO GREAT.
VADER--ANAKIN--NEVER KNEW OF HER EXISTENCE. I COULDN'T RISK THAT KNOWLEDGE FALLING INTO VADER'S HANDS.
LEIA HAS THE POTENTIAL FOR GREAT POWER IN THE FORCE--FOR GOOD OR EVIL.
HER SADNESS AND ANGER AT THE DESTRUCTION OF ALDERAAN PUT HER AT GREAT RISK TO FALL TO THE DARK SIDE.
VADER GROWS OLD. MANY GREAT WOUNDS HE HAS SUSTAINED.
AS THE EMPEROR'S SUCCESSOR, SUITABLE HE IS NOT.
ALL ALONG, THE EMPEROR HAS SOUGHT THE SON OF VADER AS HIS HEIR.
BUT THE DAUGHTER OF VADER WOULD SERVE JUST

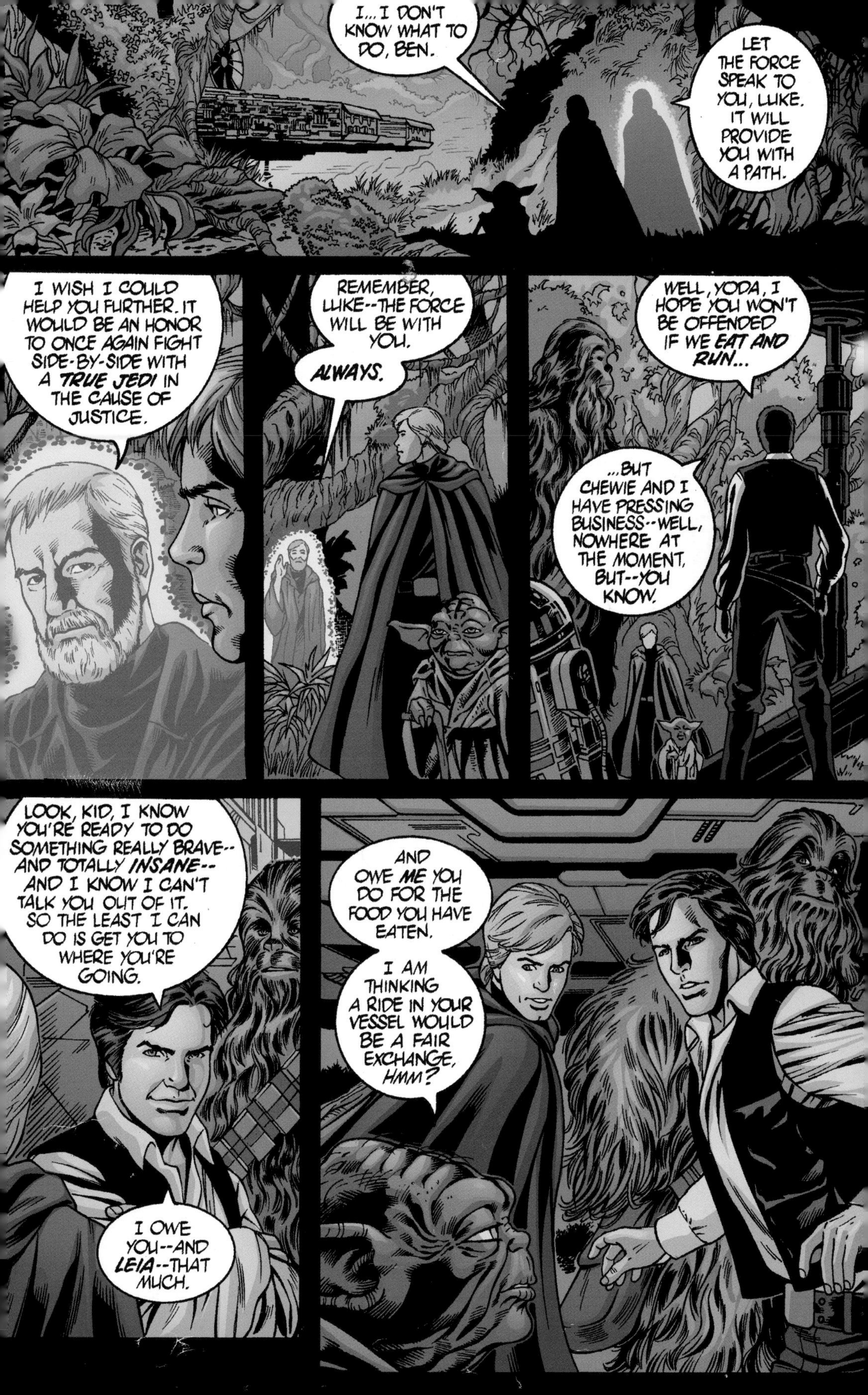
I... I DON'T KNOW WHAT TO DO, BEN.
LET THE FORCE SPEAK TO YOU, LUKE. IT WILL PROVIDE YOU WITH A PATH.
I WISH I COULD HELP YOU FURTHER. IT WOULD BE AN HONOR TO ONCE AGAIN FIGHT SIDE-BY-SIDE WITH A TRUE JEDI IN THE CAUSE OF JUSTICE.
REMEMBER, LUKE--THE FORCE WILL BE WITH YOU.
ALWAYS.
WELL, YODA, I HOPE YOU WON'T BE OFFENDED IF WE EAT AND RUN...
...BUT CHEWIE AND I HAVE PRESSING BUSINESS--WELL, NOWHERE AT THE MOMENT, BUT--YOU KNOW.
LOOK, KID, I KNOW YOU'RE READY TO DO SOMETHING REALLY BRAVE--AND TOTALLY INSANE--AND I KNOW I CAN'T TALK YOU OUT OF IT. SO THE LEAST I CAN DO IS GET YOU TO WHERE YOU'RE GOING.
I OWE YOU--AND LEIA--THAT MUCH.
AND OWE ME YOU DO FOR THE FOOD YOU HAVE EATEN.
I AM THINKING A RIDE IN YOUR VESSEL WOULD BE A FAIR EXCHANGE, HMM?

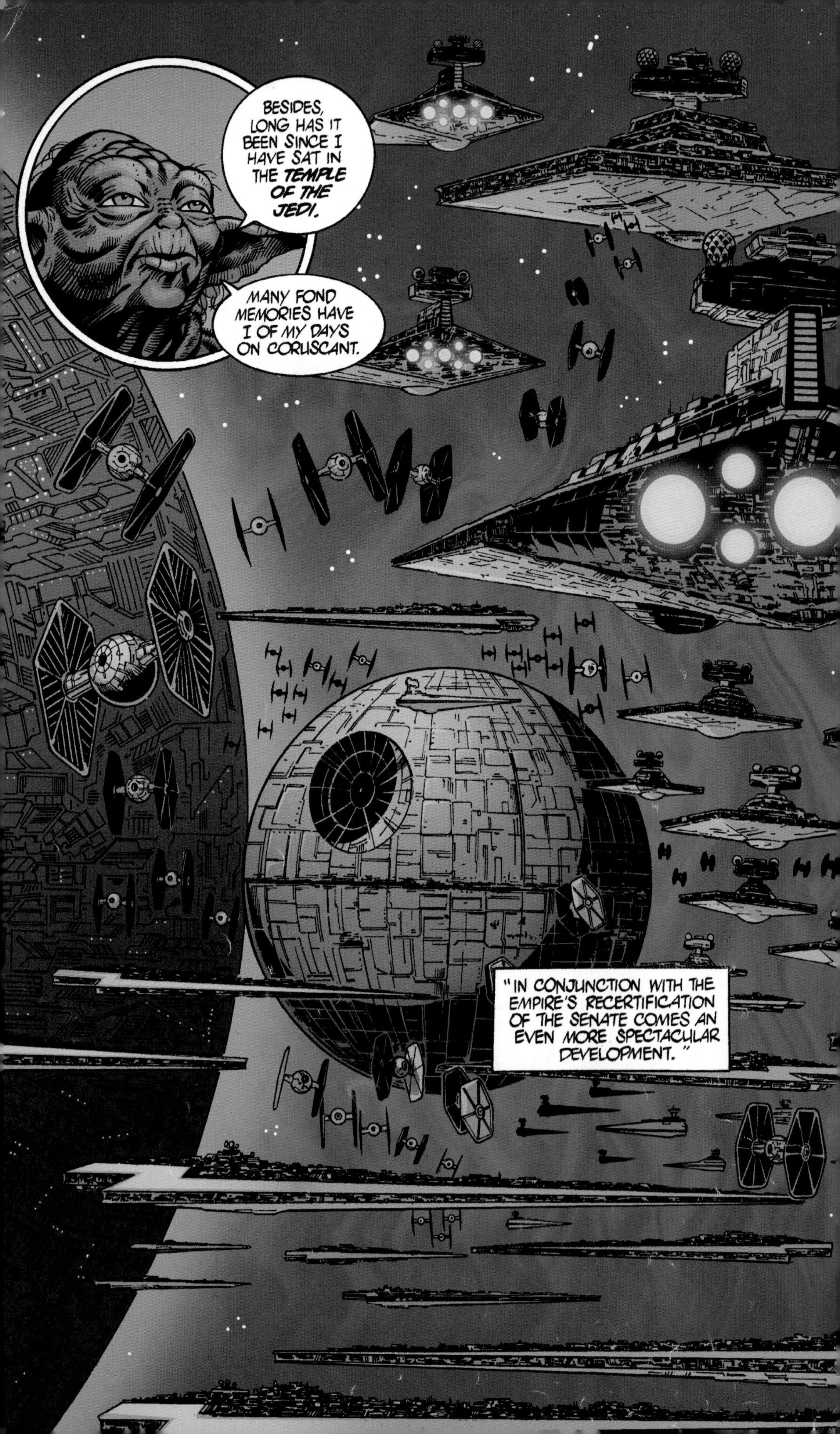
BESIDES, LONG HAS IT BEEN SINCE I HAVE SAT IN THE TEMPLE OF THE JEDI.
MANY FOND MEMORIES HAVE I OF MY DAYS ON CORUSCANT.
"IN CONJUNCTION WITH THE EMPIRE'S RECERTIFICATION OF THE SENATE COMES AN EVEN MORE SPECTACULAR DEVELOPMENT."

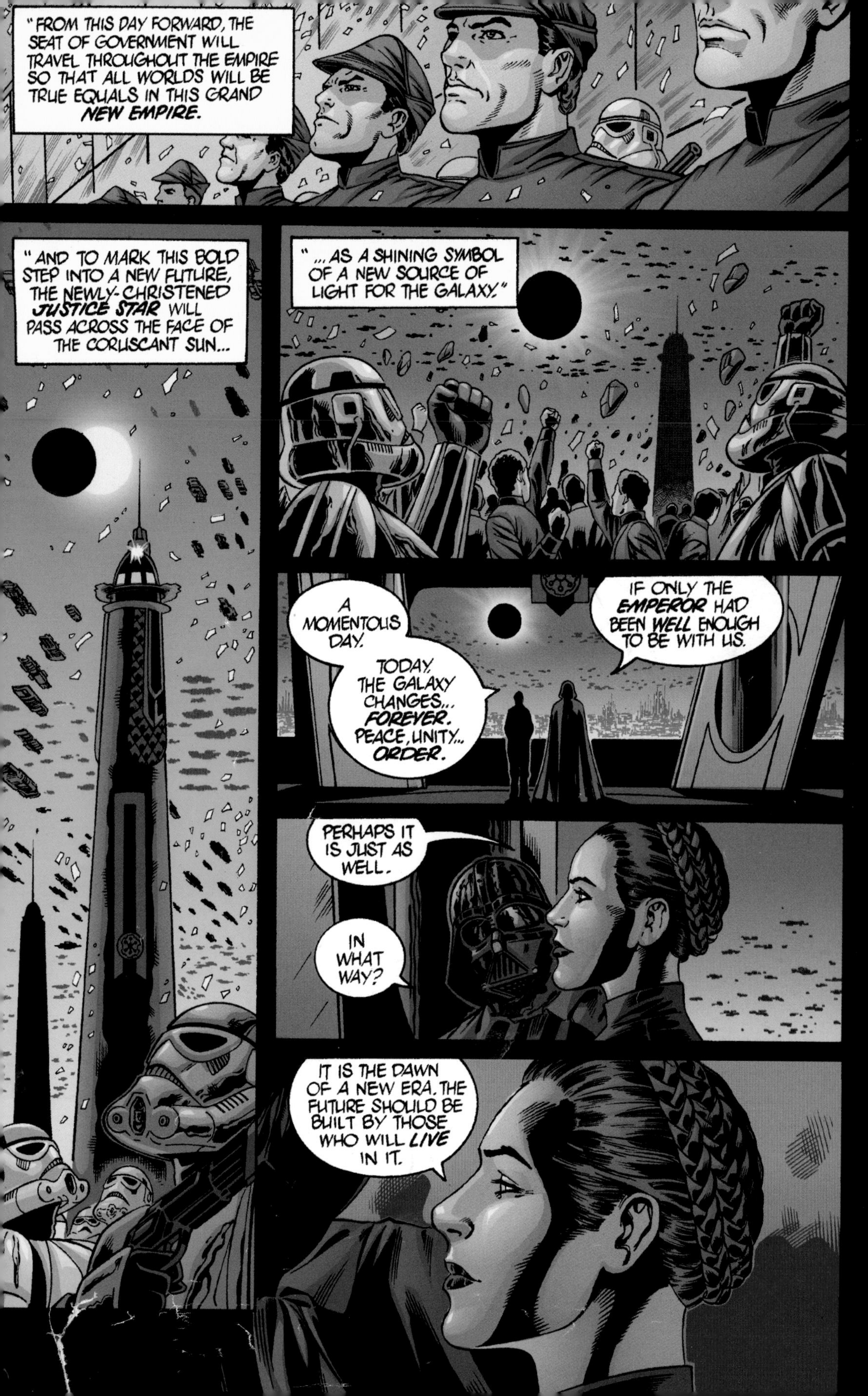
"FROM THIS DAY FORWARD, THE SEAT OF GOVERNMENT WILL TRAVEL THROUGHOUT THE EMPIRE SO THAT ALL WORLDS WILL BE TRUE EQUALS IN THIS GRAND NEW EMPIRE.
"AND TO MARK THIS BOLD STEP INTO A NEW FUTURE, THE NEWLY-CHRISTENED JUSTICE STAR WILL PASS ACROSS THE FACE OF THE CORUSCANT SUN...
"...AS A SHINING SYMBOL OF A NEW SOURCE OF LIGHT FOR THE GALAXY."
A MOMENTOUS DAY.
TODAY, THE GALAXY CHANGES... FOREVER. PEACE, UNITY... ORDER.
IF ONLY THE EMPEROR HAD BEEN WELL ENOUGH TO BE WITH US.
PERHAPS IT IS JUST AS WELL.
IN WHAT WAY?
IT IS THE DAWN OF A NEW ERA. THE FUTURE SHOULD BE BUILT BY THOSE WHO WILL LIVE IN IT.

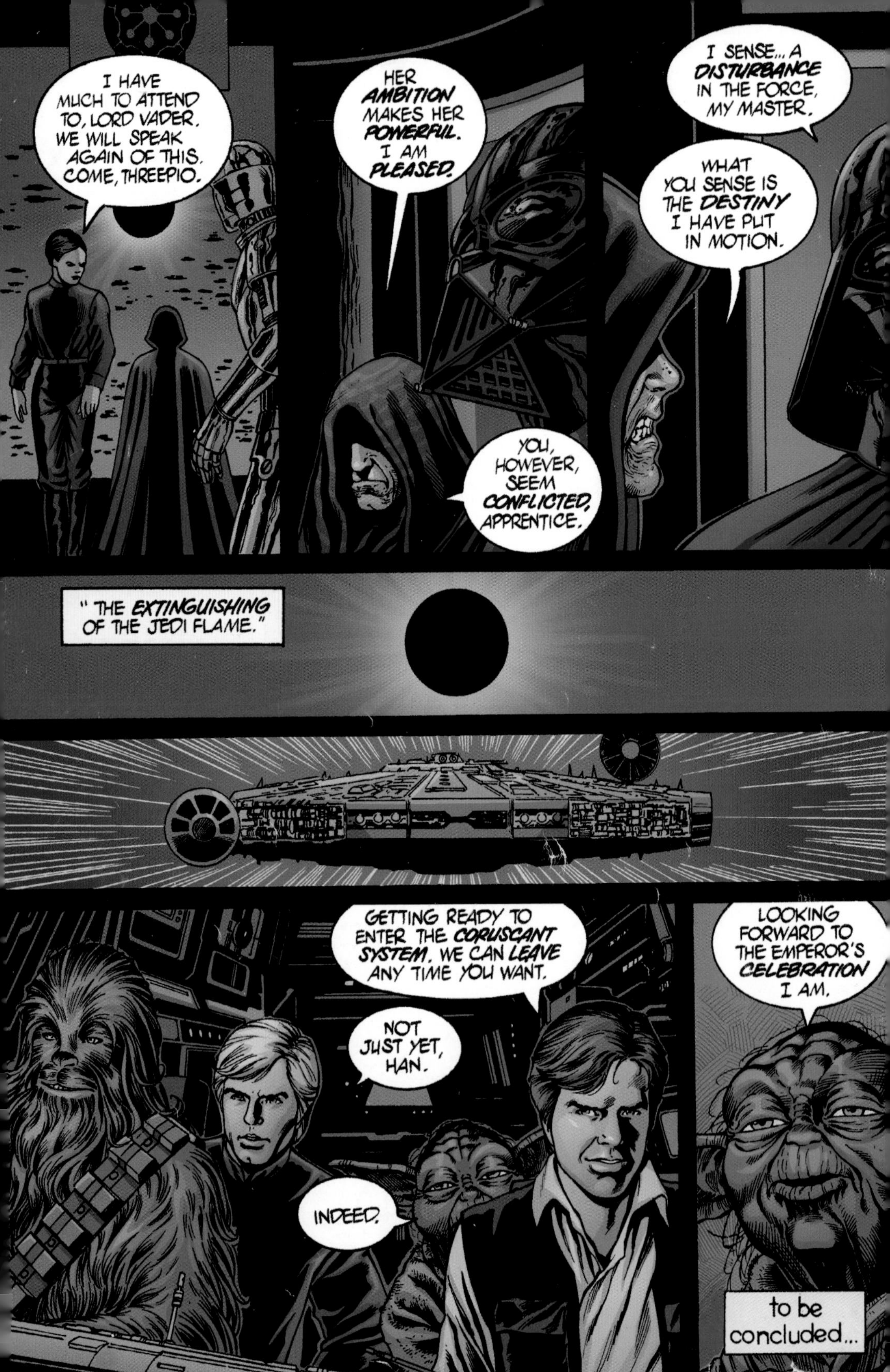
I HAVE MUCH TO ATTEND TO, LORD VADER. WE WILL SPEAK AGAIN OF THIS. COME, THREEPIO.
HER AMBITION MAKES HER POWERFUL. I AM PLEASED.
YOU, HOWEVER, SEEM CONFLICTED, APPRENTICE.
I SENSE... A DISTURBANCE IN THE FORCE, MY MASTER.
WHAT YOU SENSE IS THE DESTINY I HAVE PUT IN MOTION.
"THE EXTINGUISHING OF THE JEDI FLAME."
GETTING READY TO ENTER THE CORUSCANT SYSTEM. WE CAN LEAVE ANY TIME YOU WANT.
NOT JUST YET, HAN.
INDEED.
LOOKING FORWARD TO THE EMPEROR'S CELEBRATION I AM.
to be concluded...